PETER PAN

Walt Disney's
PETER PAN

Based on Walt Disney Productions'
full-length cartoon feature film

This adaptation by Barbara Shook Hazen
Text Illustrations by Robert Pierce

Published by WONDER BOOKS
A Division of Grosset & Dunlap, Inc.
A FILMWAYS COMPANY
Publishers • New York

TITLES IN THIS SERIES:

ALICE IN WONDERLAND
CINDERELLA
PETER PAN
PETE'S DRAGON
PINOCCHIO
SNOW WHITE AND THE SEVEN DWARFS

Copyright © 1976 Walt Disney Productions
All rights reserved.

Library of Congress Catalog Card No. 77:91870
ISBN: 0-448-16106-0
Published by Wonder Books, a Division of Grosset & Dunlap, Inc.,
by arrangement with Walt Disney Productions.
First Grosset & Dunlap Printing 1978
Printed and bound in the United States.

Adapted from the Walt Disney motion picture *Peter Pan,*
based upon *Peter Pan,* by Sir James Matthew Barrie, by arrangement
with The Hospital for Sick Children, London, England.

PETER
PAN

CHAPTER 1:
THE DARLING FAMILY

Once upon a story there lived a happy family named Darling. They lived in London in a cozy town house on a quiet street.

Wendy, John, and Michael Darling were the children. They shared the nursery—a big bedroom where they played and slept.

Wendy was the oldest. She loved games and going to the park and mending things for her brothers. Best of all she loved to tell them bedtime stories—especially stories about Peter Pan.

Peter Pan was a marvelous magic boy who lived in Never Never Land, a faraway place where mermaids, pixies, pirates, Indians, and a huge ticktocking crocodile all lived.

John and Michael loved to listen to Wendy's stories. John liked to hear about the pirates. He liked to pretend he was one.

Michael liked to hear about the Indians. He

listened with a sleepy, faraway look in his eyes. He was the baby of the family and still wore pajamas with feet in them.

Someone else shared the nursery. That someone was Nana, a large shaggy sheepdog. Nana was the children's nursemaid. She fetched and carried and watched over them as carefully as an ordinary nursemaid.

One night Wendy was telling her favorite story, the one about Peter Pan fighting Captain Hook on the deck of his own pirate ship. She was just getting to the most exciting part about Peter pretending he was a crocodile and trying to trick Captain Hook, when she heard a faint rustling in the ivy outside the nursery window. Suddenly she stopped talking.

"Don't stop now," said John breathlessly. "I so love to hear about Peter even if I know he isn't real."

The rustling grew louder. "I am *so* real," someone sitting on the window sill said.

The someone looked in.

"Why, it's Peter!" said Wendy excitedly. In his leaf-green tunic and feathered cap, she would recognize him anywhere.

Peter looked a lot like an ordinary boy. Yet he wasn't one. He was smaller and moved faster, and unlike other boys, he could fly.

Also, unlike other boys, he didn't look any particular age. That was because he would never grow up. Other children would grow up and change. But Peter wouldn't. He would always be the same Peter Pan, a happy-go-lucky magical boy.

Nana the nursemaid saw Peter Pan, too. Because her biggest job was to protect the children, she didn't like to see strangers at the nursery window.

Nana barked and sprang at the window. Her front paws hit the sash hard, and the window slammed shut.

Peter Pan darted away in the nick of time. But his shadow got caught in the closing window. It came unattached from the rest of Peter and slid inside.

Wendy quickly picked it up. She folded it carefully and put it in her dresser drawer. One thing for sure, she didn't want Nana to get her paws on it. She hoped it wouldn't get mussed. Most of all, she hoped Peter Pan would come back for it.

Nana, the faithful nursemaid, stayed at the window. She barked at the green figure till it was out of sight.

"Shush!" said Wendy. "Father will hear you. And you know how Father hates any fuss."

Wendy kept staring out the window. "I wonder what Peter was really doing here," she said.

"Maybe he likes your stories as much as we do," said John. John was a smart boy who liked to figure out the whats and whys of things.

"Oh, I hope so," said Wendy dreamily. Peter Pan was as real to her as John and Michael.

CHAPTER 2:
NURSE DOGS
AND GROWING UP

While the children were getting ready for bed, Father and Mother Darling were in their room getting ready to go to a party.

"George dear, do hurry," said Mother Darling. "We mustn't be late, you know."

"I do know," said Father Darling. He was banging dresser drawers open and shut. "But unless I find my cuff links, we don't go to the party."

Father Darling said a loud "Ouch!"

"Ouch what?" asked Mother Darling sweetly.

Father Darling didn't answer. He hopped about on one foot and held his head. He hopped because one of the dresser drawers had fallen on his foot. He held his head because of all the noise coming from the nursery.

"I'm going in there right now," said Father Darling. And he did.

What he saw didn't help his head or his temper.

11

John and Michael were dueling on John's bed.

Little Michael was playing the part of Peter Pan. And John was playing the part of Captain Hook, the head of the wicked pirates.

"Take that!" Michael shouted. He waved his paper sword and asked, "Give up?"

"Never!" said John firmly. He slashed the air with a coat hanger that he held in his right hand. "I'll teach you to cut off me right hand," he shouted.

"No, John," corrected Wendy. "It was Hook's left hand that Peter Pan cut off. That's how he got his name—because of the sharp hook he put in its place."

"I see," said John, switching the coat hanger. What John didn't see was his father.

He bumped into him just as Michael was advancing and calling out, "Take that, you old bilge rat!"

Father Darling fell on a pile of fallen toys and blocks. His face was red, and he was furious.

"Now see here, Michael," he sputtered, "what do you mean by calling me. . . ."

"Not you, Father," John tried to explain. "Me. I'm the one Michael's calling an old bilge rat. You see I'm Captain Hook and Michael's Peter Pan and . . . ."

"What I want to know," said Father Darling, "is

who's at the bottom of this and where are my cuff links."

"Cuff links?" said Michael. There was a funny look on his face.

"Maybe they're on the treasure map," whispered John just as Father Darling saw something under John's bed.

"What I'd like to know is what my dress shirt front is doing here?" said Father Darling. "And why there are chalk marks all over it?"

Little Michael jumped up and down. "Hooray for Father. He found the treasure map. Now we can look for the treasure. Can't we, Wendy?"

Wendy didn't answer. She took out her handkerchief and wiped the chalk marks off her father's shirt front."

"See," she said. "They come right off."

Father Darling gave his daughter a dark look. "Wendy, I want to have a serious talk with you," he said. "I want you to stop stuffing the boys' heads with a lot of silly stories."

"But they weren't silly, Father," said Wendy. Her eyes grew wide.

"I say they are!" said Father Darling. "All these goings-on with Captain Crook and Peter Pirate . . . ."

"Captain Hook and Peter Pan," corrected Wendy.

". . . are pure nonsense," continued Father Darling. "It's pure poppycock!"

"Now, George," said Mrs. Darling as she came into the room. She always tried to smooth things over.

"Now George, nothing!" said Father Darling. It was clear he was in a bad mood. "Wendy's growing up. She's getting too old for silly stories and childish fiddle-faddle. This is her last night in the nursery."

Wendy looked as if her heart might break. "You don't mean it?" she asked.

"I *do* mean it," said Father Darling in his sternest voice. "Besides it's a bad influence on the boys. This is your last night. And that is my last word on the subject."

As Father Darling started out the door, he stepped on Nana's tail.

Nana yelped and jumped into the children's wagon. It careened round and round with her in it and crashed into bookshelves and blocks and piles of clothes.

"Poor Nana!" said the children.

"Poor Nana indeed!" boomed Father Darling.

When he was mad at one thing, he often was mad at everything. "And that's another thing," he said. "Nana is a dog even if she is your nursemaid. I've had enough! Tonight Nana sleeps in the yard."

Father Darling pulled Nana out the door and down the front steps. He tried not to hear the children's pleas of "Please, please. Don't take Nana away."

He could see the sad look in Nana's big brown eyes as he tied her to a tree in the front yard.

"Try to understand," said Father Darling. "You *are* a nursemaid, but, well, you're *really* a dog. And the children are children, not little puppies. And sooner or later children have to grow up and become grown-ups. And there's just too much commotion in the nursery. And. . . ."

Father Darling paused. He thought he heard someone laughing in the distance. It didn't sound like one of his children so he didn't think twice about it. If only he'd known more about Peter Pan, he would have looked up.

Upstairs in the nursery, Wendy and her mother were talking about growing up, too. "I don't ever want to grow up!" said Wendy. "Never ever!"

"Father called Peter Pan poppy-something," said John sadly. He was already in his nightshirt in bed and his glasses, top hat and umbrella were by the bedside table, ready for the next day.

Mother Darling tried to comfort the children. "I'm sure your father didn't mean everything he

16

said," she said. "He's just upset because he can't find his good cuff links, and. . . ."

Suddenly Michael sat up in bed. He stared at something under the teddy bear on his pillow.

"What is it, dear?" asked Mother Darling.

"The buried treasure," said Michael. "I guess I forgot." He held up his father's gold cuff links.

Mother Darling took them and gave Michael a hug.

As they walked to the door, she blew all the children a kiss. "Please don't judge your father too harshly," she said. "He loves all of you very much. Now get a good night's sleep."

Mother Darling started to turn the lock.

Wendy rose up in her bed. "Please don't lock it, mother," she said. "*He* might come back."

"He?" Mother Darling looked puzzled. "Why would your father. . . ."

"Not Father," said Wendy with a strange smile. "Peter Pan. You see I found something that belongs to him."

"What is that?" asked Mother Darling. Wendy's words stirred something in her. Mother Darling had believed in Peter Pan when she was a little girl.

"His shadow," said Wendy. "Peter was here, and Nana chased him away and closed the window, but his shadow got caught, and I grabbed it. And I'm

18

keeping it for him."

"Where? What do you mean?" Mother Darling wanted to know more.

Wendy didn't answer. She was already asleep. So Mother Darling tiptoed out of the nursery and on down the stairs.

CHAPTER 3:
PETER RETURNS

At last Mother and Father Darling were on their way to the party. Mother Darling was worried. "Are you sure the children will be safe in the nursery without Nana there?" she asked.

"Of course," said Father Darling. "Why wouldn't they be safe?"

Mother Darling paused and glanced back at the house. "Well," she said, "Wendy said something about Peter Pan's shadow. I wish I knew what she meant."

Father Darling couldn't resist teasing her. "You don't say," he said in a mock scared voice. "What shall we do? Perhaps we should sound an alarm? Or call the police?"

"Please be serious," said Mother Darling. "There must be something to it. Nana seemed upset when we left."

"Oh, Mary," said Father Darling a bit crossly.

"Of all the impossible childish fiddle-faddle. Peter Pan isn't real. He's just a lot of foolishness. And you shouldn't clutter your head with such nonsense."

"Whatever you say, dear," said Mother Darling. They walked on, but she was still worried.

It was a good thing Mother Darling didn't look up. For there was Peter Pan *himself* perched right on their rooftop. He heard every word and almost laughed out loud when Father Darling called him "childish fiddle-faddle."

Peter was not alone. His pixie friend Tinker Bell was with him. She was a tiny creature with white shiny wings and golden hair.

She was so small, sometimes all you could see of her was her glow. She sparkled because there was a magic light deep inside her. And because she was a pixie, she tinkled instead of talked. Only Peter Pan knew the meaning of her words.

And right now she was saying to Peter, "Aren't people silly." To anyone else it would sound like the tune of tiny bells.

Peter nodded. Then he signaled to Tinker Bell to "Follow me."

The two of them flew straight to the nursery window sill. Peter lifted the window and they slipped inside.

The glow of Tinker Bell's magic light made it

easy to see. Wendy, John and Michael were all asleep in their beds.

Peter pointed to Nana's empty doghouse. "Over there," he said. "Is it over there?"

It was clear Peter was looking for something. Tinker Bell flitted over and looked inside. "No," she shook her tiny head. "It's not in there."

Peter looked disappointed. "My shadow has to be somewhere," he said. "I've just got to find it."

Peter started searching in the children's toy chest and calling, "Shadow, oh, shadow, where are you? Come back to me, shadow."

He pulled out blocks and books and cars and trucks and stuffed animals and pull toys. He did not find anything that looked the least bit like his shadow.

"Please help me find my shadow," Peter Pan said to Tinker Bell. She was smiling at herself and doing figure eights in front of the mirror.

Tinker Bell flew about. After a few minutes, she pointed to the top drawer of Wendy's chest. "It's in there," she tinkled. She knew because she could see it through the keyhole.

Tinker Bell put her arms to her sides and flew in through the keyhole.

Peter pulled the drawer open and tried to grab his shadow. But it didn't want to come back right away. It slipped under Wendy's bed and slid to the other side of the nursery.

In his excitement he slammed the drawer shut so hard that everything inside got all jumbled. The keyhole was blocked by Wendy's things. Tinker Bell was trapped inside and couldn't get back out.

"Let me out! Let me out!" Tinker Bell tinkled to Peter Pan.

Peter was too busy chasing his shadow to hear her. Every time he got near it, it scooted just out of reach. It slipped down walls and slid under the rug. It quite liked being on its own.

"I'll get you, wait and see!" Peter called to his shadow. He flew to the ceiling light and pounced on it.

He was quick. But his shadow was quicker. It oozed out of reach.

Peter saw the toe tip of his shadow by the washstand. Again he pounced. This time he grabbed its big toe.

Clinging to his shadow, Peter slid across the polished floor. The washstand fell over with a loud crash!

Wendy woke up and rubbed her sleepy eyes. She thought she was dreaming because she saw Peter Pan.

Then she saw the fallen washstand and knew it was true. "Oh, Peter," Wendy called out excitedly. "I hoped you'd come back. I saved your shadow for you. I hope it didn't get rumpled in the drawer."

Peter was sitting on his shadow. It was still squiggling and wriggling, and Peter was trying to stick his real foot into his shadow foot. He didn't know quite how to do it. He was rubbing his real foot with a bar of soap that had been in the washstand, hoping that would work.

Wendy walked over to him. "Peter Pan," she laughed. "You may know a lot. But you don't know how to put on a shadow. You can't stick it on with

28

soap. It'll slip right off. what a shadow need is sewing."

Peter grinned, "I never thought of that."

Wendy went to her chest of drawers where she kept her clean underwear, her hair ribbons and her sewing things.

Inside the drawer she saw a strange eerie glow. It was Tinker Bell, but Wendy didn't know that. They hadn't met yet.

When she opened the drawer, Tinker Bell wooshed out, tinkling angrily. She didn't like being locked up in a clutter of needles and pins and thread spools.

Tinker Bell shook her magic wand at Peter. Then she glared at Wendy and tinkled again loudly.

"Who's that?" asked Wendy. "And what is she saying?"

"That's Tinker Bell," said Peter. "She's a pixie, and she's my best friend. She talks in a magic way I can understand her.

"What she's saying," said Peter, "is that she thinks you're a big, ugly girl and she doesn't think she's going to like you."

"What a shame," said Wendy softly. "I like her. And I'd like to have wings."

"Tink gets terribly jealous," said Peter. That was all he said, but Wendy couldn't help feeling it was too bad Tinker Bell didn't like her.

Wendy sat on Peter's feet and sewed on his shadow. She took small, careful stitches.

"I'm so glad you came back," said Wendy. "Most of all, I'm glad you like my stories about you."

"Oh I do!" said Peter. "So do all the Lost Boys!"

"Who are they?" asked Wendy.

Peter explained, "The Lost Boys live in Never Never Land. They had fallen out of their carriages and were lost when they were babies. They have no homes. But they love stories, and I take yours back to them."

"I'm glad," said Wendy. She thought how awful it would be not to have a home.

"Another thing," said Peter Pan. "The Lost Boys will never grow up."

Wendy started sobbing.

"What's the matter?" asked Peter. "Did I say something wrong?"

"No," said Wendy, shaking her head. "It's just that I have to start growing up tomorrow. Tonight's my last night in the nursery. Father said so."

"Does that mean no more stories?" asked Peter.

"That's just what it means," said Wendy. She wiped her tears and bit off the sewing thread. At least Peter Pan and his shadow were back together again.

30

Peter took a few springy steps and crowed with delight.

He saw how sad Wendy was and pulled her toward the nursery window. "Come with me, Wendy," said Peter Pan.

"Wh-wh-where?" sobbed Wendy.

"To Never Never Land," crowed Peter. "That's the place to go where you'll never have to grow up."

CHAPTER 4:
ON THEIR WAY

"**I**t sounds wonderful," said Wendy. She took a few steps. Then she pulled back.

"Wait a minute," said Wendy with a frown. "I can't go. What would my mother say?"

"Mother?" said Peter. He sounded puzzled. "What's a mother?"

Wendy was shocked. "Why Peter Pan, you mean to tell me you don't know what a mother is?" she said.

Peter shook his head.

"A mother," said Wendy, "is someone who loves you and cares for you and looks after you."

Peter still looked puzzled.

"And tells you stories," Wendy added.

Peter smiled, "That sounds like the best part. In Never Never Land you can tell stories to the Lost Boys."

Wendy hesitated. She was very excited and a little afraid. "I can't go without Michael and John," she said.

"Bring them along," said Peter brightly.

That settled it. Wendy rushed over to John's bed. "John! John!" she called as she tugged at his covers. "Peter Pan is here. He really is here!"

John sat up in bed and reached for his glasses.

"Wow!" he said when he put them on. For it clearly was Peter Pan himself in his leafy clothes and feathered cap.

Next Wendy woke up Michael. He was too sleepy to say anything but, "Hello, I'm Michael."

As he rubbed the sleep from his eyes, he saw something small and glowing sitting on Peter Pan's shoulder.

"Look!" Michael whispered to the others. "A firefly!"

Tinker Bell didn't like being called a bug. Not even a nice bug like a firefly. Just out of mischief, she pulled Michael's hair.

"Ouch!" said Michael. "That firefly's no fun."

Very carefully, Wendy explained that Tinker Bell was a pixie, a special kind of magic creature, and not any kind of bug.

"What's the pixie saying?" asked Michael. He heard the tiny tinkling noise she was making.

"She's saying it's time to go to Never Never

Land," said Peter. He pointed out the window to the moon and stars.

John was ready. He had everything he needed—his glasses, his top hat and his umbrella in case of rain. He was still in his nightshirt but that didn't bother him, or anyone else.

Michael was ready, too. He had his teddy bear, which was all he needed.

John was jumping up and down on his bed fencing imaginary pirates. "I can't wait," he said. "I've never crossed swords with *real* pirates."

"Just one thing," said Peter, getting serious. "If you come with me, you've got to take orders. And leave Captain Hook to me. We've been after each other a long time."

"Aye, aye, sir," said John with a snappy salute.

Wendy was worrying. "How do we get to Never Never Land?" she asked Peter.

"We fly, of course," crowed Peter. "That's the only way."

"But I can't fly," said Wendy. "I don't know how." She looked at Peter sadly.

"Sure you do," said Peter. "You can fly. All you have to do is try."

Peter flew around the room, from Wendy's bed to the washstand and back again.

"Maybe you can do that," said Wendy glumly.

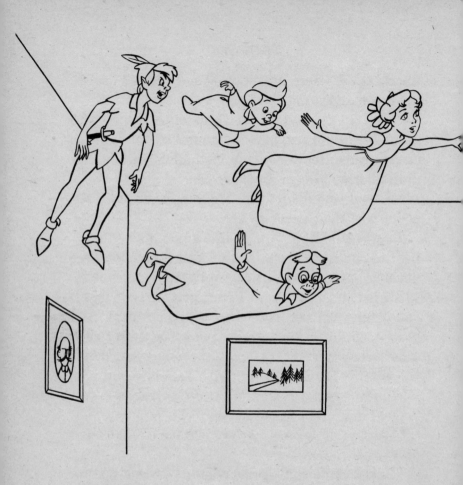

"But *I* can't."

"Yes, you can," said Peter. "All you do is think happy thoughts."

"Like getting toys at Christmas?" said Wendy hopefully.

Peter nodded. "Now you've got the idea."

"Or sleighbells or snow or going sledding?" said John excitedly.

"Exactly!" crowed Peter Pan. Then he added shyly, "My happy thought is having all of you come to Never Never Land with me. Now let's practice."

Peter took Wendy's hand, and Wendy took John's hand, and John took Michael's hand. At first they took small flights—from bed to bed and bureau to bureau.

Then, as the children's thoughts got happier, they got braver. They started flying higher and higher.

Soon they were sailing gaily around the nursery, touching all four corners and swinging from the ceiling light. They did twists and turns and even "loop the loops."

"Oh, this is fun!" cried Wendy. "I feel free as a bird."

"See," said Peter Pan. "I told you so. You *can* fly. It's easier than pie."

Now Tinker Bell played the first of her pranks on Wendy. She sprinkled the air with pixie dust. This made everyone go faster.

"Whee!" said John, as tables, chairs, bookshelves, beds and toys whizzed by in a blur.

"Stop!" cried Wendy. Everything was whirling by too fast for her. She felt dizzy.

37

"Please," she asked Peter. "Let's rest a second."

"Well, just a second," said Peter. "It's time we're on our way."

After Wendy caught her breath, Peter said, "Now all join hands again and think your happiest thoughts."

Wendy closed her eyes tight and pressed Peter's hand. "I'm thinking of a mermaid lagoon under a magic moon," she said.

"I'm thinking of a pirate cave," said John as he grabbed on to Wendy's hand.

"I'm thinking I'm an Indian brave," said little Michael. He held on to John with both hands.

Then, as they thought, they soared right out the nursery window into the night. Now they were really on their way to Never Never Land.

"Look up!" said Wendy happily. "See the stars and the man in the moon. They all seem to be winking at me."

"I've never seen anything so beautiful," said Wendy. She gave Peter's hand a squeeze.

"Look down!" said John. "That's even better. I see our chimney and the church steeple and all the streetlights. Everything looks so much brighter and better from up here."

"Let me show you some really interesting sights," said Peter Pan gleefully. He led the children on a merry tour of London.

First they dipped down and followed the winding River Thames. It was fun to wink back at the lights on the little river boats.

Then they swooped down and saw London Bridge, the Tower of London, and all the other tourist sights.

Most exciting of all was landing right on Big Ben. Peter Pan stood face to face with the famous clock. Just for mischief, he moved the minute hand and made the bells chime.

"Do it again," begged Wendy. So Peter did.

"Oh," said Wendy, flapping her arms, "I don't want to grow up—ever."

"I never will!" said Peter Pan.

Nana the nursemaid overheard. She was still tied up in the Darling's front yard. Her paws were over her eyes, and she was sulking. What if something terrible happened to the children while she was not in the nursery!

When Nana heard Wendy's voice, she peeked. She thought she saw Wendy sitting in her nightgown on a fleecy cloud.

She blinked, then looked again. This time she thought she saw John and Michael doing somersaults and back flips in the sky. She was sure it was John. No one else had a top hat like his.

Nana whimpered softly. The children were her responsibility, and she was helpless. She flopped her big ears.

It was no use. *She* couldn't fly. The rope was strong, and her feet stayed firmly on the ground.

Now Nana heard the children singing:

When there's a smile in your heart,
There's no better time to start.
Think of all the joy you'll find
When you leave the world behind.

Nana did not feel one bit joyous. Worst of all, she saw that the perky person leading the children farther and farther away was Peter Pan himself.

CHAPTER 5:
PIRATE COVE

While Peter Pan and the children were flying straight to Never Never Land, Captain Hook was pacing the floor of his pirate ship. There was a frown on his wicked face. He was thinking about Peter Pan.

"Blast that Peter Pan," Captain Hook muttered as he studied his pirate map. "Where is he anyway? I'd have had him by now if only I knew what part of Never Never Land his hideout is in. But, by my blarmy, I haven't the foggiest notion."

"Mermaid Lagoon?" suggested Smee. Smee was Captain Hook's first mate. He was bald, roly-poly, and a bumbler. He never meant to be a pirate. Once, because of his bad eyes, he got on the wrong ship. And he never got off.

"No," said Captain Hook, who always asked Smee's advice but rarely took it. "We've searched Mermaid Lagoon."

"Cannibal Cove?" Smee then suggested.

"We've combed Cannibal Cove," said Captain Hook with a wave of his hook hand.

He banged the hook down hard on the pirate map—so hard it ripped the paper, right up to Indian Camp.

"Is that where you're pointing?" asked Smee in a small voice.

"No, no, no!" roared the hot-tempered Hook. He walked away from the map table.

"But wait!" Captain Hook stopped and stroked his chin. "That gives me an idea. Those Indians know this island better than I do my own ship. I wonder."

"Wonder what?" asked Smee, edging closer.

Captain Hook clicked his heels together. "Tiger Lily," he said. Then he roared with laughter.

"T-T-T-Tiger Lily, Captain?" said Smee. He stuttered when he didn't understand, which was often.

Captain Hook glared at his first mate. "The chief's idiot daughter," he said. "I mean, the chief's daughter, Idiot."

Hook tapped Smee on the tip of his nose. "She'll know where Peter Pan hides out," he said.

Smee still had the shakes. Captain Hook had a way of making him feel nervous. "B-b-but will

Tiger Lily talk?'' he asked.

Captain Hook smiled his evil, oily smile. "With a little persuasion, perhaps," he said. "Now let me see. Do you think boiling in oil is little enough? Or dragging Tiger Lily from the back of the boat? Or leaving her on Marooner's Rock with a lot of crocodiles?"

Marooner's Rock was a small rocky island right

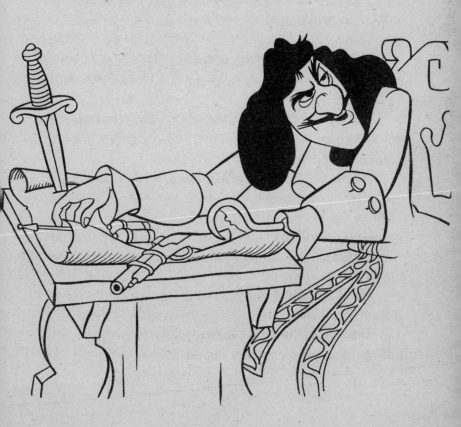

off Never Never Land. It was where mutinous pirates were left to die. When the tide rose, the island was covered with water and they were washed out to sea. It was a terrible way to die.

And Captain Hook had a terrible fear of crocodiles. Even saying the word made him turn pale. That was because of the big crocodile that once ate Captain Hook's left hand. The crocodile liked the taste of the pirate captain so much he followed him everywhere. He wanted the rest of him, too.

Beads of perspiration stood on Captain Hook's forehead. "Thank goodness for the clock," he said to Smee.

"Aye, aye, sir," said Smee. "Throwing that alarm clock in the crocodile's mouth was a smart move, Captain."

"Of course," said Captain Hook with a sly sneer. Actually he'd thrown the clock because it was the only thing he had in his hand. But ever since the crocodile swallowed it, the croc ticked and tocked like a clock. At least Captain Hook knew when the crocodile was around.

"If it weren't for the tick and the tock he'd have had me by now," said the Captain with a shudder. Thinking about the crocodile made him forget all about his plan to capture Tiger Lily.

"I think a shave might make me feel better," said Captain Hook to his first mate. He sank into his barber's chair. Captain Hook was a brave man—except where the crocodile was concerned.

It was like a bad dream coming true. Captain Hook heard a low tick-tock, tick-tock while he was being lathered up.

Suddenly, all soapy and slippery, he leaped into Smee's arms. "Save me! Oh, save me!" the Captain cried out. "Don't let the croc get me."

Soon as he said it, Captain Hook was ashamed. What was the wickedest pirate captain in the world doing sniveling in his first mate's arms?

"By my blarmy," said Captain Hook, recovering his calm. "Let's do away with that beast once and for all. Let's blast him to blazes.

"Follow me," Hook called to Smee. He hurried out of the cabin and ran up on deck.

There the busy pirates were swabbing the deck and polishing the brass and singing:

Oh a pirate's life is a wonderful life,
A roaring over the sea.
Give me a career as a buccaneer.
It's the life of a pirate for me.

Yes, a pirate's life is a wonderful life.
They never bury your bones.
For when it's all over, a jolly sea rover
drops in on his friend, Davy Jones.

Captain Hook interrupted their singing. "To arms!" he ordered. "Ready pistols. Man the Long Tom." The latter was a cannon, the largest on the ship. It shot cannon balls the size of basketballs.

"Aye, aye," said the crew eagerly. The men were delighted. They didn't like it when the ship just sat around collecting barnacles. They liked action. Now the men sang out, "Yo-ho, heave-ho, a shooting we will go."

Captain Hook leaned over the ship's railing. In the distant waters, the crocodile was lurking. Its tongue was hanging out. Its tail tail thumped and kept time to the ticks and tocks of its internal clock.

"Double the powder and shorten the fuse," the Captain bellowed. "Blow the crocodile to bits!"

He looked through the telescope just to double-check the croc's position. That was when he spotted the four flying figures, directly north of the crocodile's snout.

The one in front wore green and had a long feather in his cap. "Peter Pan, me arch enemy," said Captain Hook. "I'd recognize him anywere. Swoggle me eyes. What's he doing with three scummy looking brats?!"

It was the chance of a lifetime. "Shorten the powder and double the fuse," the Captain changed his orders. "We'll kill off the crocodile later."

Right now what the wicked pirate wanted was to shoot down Peter Pan.

CHAPTER 6:
AFTER THE WENDY BIRD

Happily Peter Pan and the children were unaware of any danger as they were flying full speed to Never Never Land.

The closer they flew, the clearer they could see. "It's just the way I always thought it would be," said Wendy excitedly. "Look! There's Mermaid Lagoon. See how the waters shine. Everything looks strange—yet so familiar. It's like coming home after a holiday."

John looked down at all the dark unexplored patches on the Island. He squinted hard at one. "I see the Indian Camp," he called out.

"And I see Captain Hook and his pirates," said Michael. He didn't sound worried though. He was taking it easy. He was lying on his stomach and letting a little cloud carry him.

The second Michael said, "Captain Hook" there was a loud boom! A cannon ball cut through the

clouds and just missed Michael's left foot.

Boom! Another cannon ball burst through the air. The wind from it almost blew off John's top hat. "What's going on?" asked John.

Peter Pan was too busy dodging cannon balls to answer right away. He looked worried, which was not at all like Peter.

He turned to Tinker Bell. "Quick, Tink," said Peter. "Take Wendy and the boys to the Island. I'll stay here and draw Captain Hook's fire. Imagine treating guests to Never Never Land so badly!"

Tinker Bell answered Peter with a loud jingle and a shrug. She waggled her finger at Wendy to follow after her.

Wendy and the boys had a hard time keeping up.

"Not so fast, please," panted Wendy, out of breath. Peter never went so fast. Wendy didn't like it.

But Tinker Bell didn't care. She speeded up even more. She was angry at Wendy and angry at Peter. She didn't want Wendy in Never Never Land. She wanted Peter all to herself—the way it had been. And she thought of a nasty trick to play to get rid of Wendy.

"Please wait!" Wendy wailed.

Tinker Bell jangled and jingled and flitted out of sight.

"I don't think Tinker Bell wants to," said John. "I don't think she likes you. She's jealous because Peter likes you."

"Nonsense," said Wendy. But she wasn't entirely sure it was.

Tinker Bell had already landed on a mushroom stoop in Mermaid Lagoon. She rested a bit and waved to a friendly flamingo with a broken leg. Then she flitted through the low leaves to a knothole door.

The door led into a tree trunk that led down to a secret cave. This was the entrance to the Camp of the Lost Boys.

They were boys who had no families. They lived

in the cave and wore animal skins instead of regular
clothing. They were the boys who had been lost as
babies and would never grow up.

Tinker Bell flew through the bedroom with all the
bunk beds in it. First she tried to wake up Tubby, a

roly-poly boy with a curly cowlick. Tubby didn't budge.

Then Tinker Bell took a wooden club down from the wall and bonked Foxy on his head. Foxy was the leader of the boys, and the one Tink could most count on to help her play her dirty trick.

"What's up?" said Foxy in a sleepy, snarly voice. He shook the two forms in the next bunk beds.

This woke up the twins. "Who do you think you're shoving?" asked the one.

"Yes, who do you think?" said the other.

"You, that's who," said Foxy.

By now all the Lost Boys were awake. And all were scrapping and fighting and in bad moods.

Tinker Bell frowned. She pulled Foxy's hair and tinkled something in his ear.

Foxy looked startled. "Huh?" he said. "You mean *those* are Peter Pan's orders?"

Tinker Bell nodded.

Foxy raised both hands. "Hold it, boys," he called out. "Cut the fighting. Tink has orders from Peter. And you know what that means."

What it meant was the boys would do anything Peter Pan asked. He was their hero.

"What are the orders?" asked Tubby.

Foxy told them. "Tink says a terrible creature called a Wendy Bird is on her way here. A big, ugly

creature from another land. . . ."

Tinker Bell jingled and jangled.

"And Peter wants us to get rid of the Wendy Bird," said Foxy. As he said it, he shook his fist.

"Smash it, you mean?" asked Cubby.

"Kick it, maybe?" said Tubby.

"Step on it? Step on it?" suggested the twins. Because the Lost Boys didn't grow up with loving

families, their ways were not gentle. They didn't know how to behave because they had no mother to teach them.

Tinker Bell held out her tiny arms as if she were shooting a gun.

"I got it," said all the Lost Boys together. "Shoot it down. That's what Peter wants."

Tink smiled smugly. She twinkled and waved for

everyone to follow her.

"Let's go. Let's go." They all rushed out of the cave with their weapons—rocks and sling shots and paper wads and squirt guns. Whatever Peter Pan wanted, they were there to do.

They ran all the way to Vantage Point, the highest point in Never Never Land. That was where they would wait for the Wendy Bird.

Minutes passed. Tinker Bell pointed at a spot in the sky. As the spot came closer, it grew larger and girl-shaped.

"I see the Wendy Bird," called Foxy.

"Me, too. Me, too," said the twins.

The boys got out their weapons. Foxy gave the orders. "Ready. Aim . . . Fire!"

Zip! Whiz! Woosh! Rocks and paper wads rushed by Wendy. One caught the hem of her gown and ripped it.

"Help!" screamed Wendy. In reaching for her gown, she let go of John's hand.

Then she completely lost her balance and started to fall down, down, down.

"Somebody help me, please," screamed Wendy. She was hurtling toward the ground at a tremendous speed. Below she could see some jagged rocks. She closed her eyes, crossed her fingers, and prepared herself for the worst.

The next thing she knew, two strong arms were around her steadying her course. They belonged to Peter Pan, who had heard Wendy's screams. Quick as magic he had sped to Vantage Point and caught her just above the rocks.

Wendy clung to Peter as they floated to earth. "Thank you, Peter Pan," said Wendy, giving him a grateful hug. "You saved my life."

"Are you sure you're all right?" asked John, rushing over to Wendy. He and Michael had already landed. When Wendy fell, John simply opened his umbrella, and the two of them parachuted safely to Never Never Land.

All the Lost Boys circled around. "Hi, Peter," they called out. "What's up? We were just following your orders."

"Yeah!" said Foxy, stepping forward. "We were just trying to shoot down the Wendy Bird like you said . . . And I almost got it with my skull-buster here."

"Me, too. Me, too," said the twins.

Peter put his hands on his hips. "Attention!" he shouted. He looked angry.

"What I want to say," Peter said, "is that you are all a bunch of blockheads!" Peter spat out the last word.

He paced back and forth in front of the boys.

"Fine thing. I bring you a mother to tell you stories and . . . ."

"A mother?" said Foxy with a puzzled look. "What's a mother?"

"And you try to shoot her down," Peter continued.

Then he tried to explain what a mother is. "Someone who loves you and tells you stories, who sews on buttons and tucks you in bed at night," said Peter Pan.

Cubby and Tubby started to cry. Like all the Lost Boys, they wanted to please Peter. And it was obvious Peter was not a bit pleased.

"Aw, shucks!" said Cubby. "A mother sounds like a nice thing to have. I like stories."

"Tink said that Wendy was a bird," said Tubby. "And she said *you* said to shoot it down."

"Come here!" Peter called to Tinker Bell, who had been hiding and sulking in a flower.

Tink kicked the flower petals and flew over to Peter. Her light was a blazing, angry glimmer.

"I charge you with high treason," Peter pointed his finger at Tinker Bell. "Do you plead guilty or not?"

Tinker Bell turned her back and shrugged saucily.

"Don't you know you might have killed Wendy?"

said Peter. He sounded concerned.

Tinker Bell couldn't help smiling. She didn't answer.

Peter looked Tink straight in the eye. "Because you won't give me an answer and because of what you've done, I banish you forever from Never Never Land," he said.

Tinker Bell stamped her tiny pixie feet and glared at Peter. Then she flew away.

"Please, Peter," Wendy pulled at his arm. "Don't be so hard on Tinker Bell. It isn't all her fault. She can't help being jealous. And no punishment should be forever. Why, that's father away than Christmas!"

"Well, then, one week," said Peter, softening. "Now come with me, Wendy. I'm going to take you on a special tour of the Island."

CHAPTER 7:
ONWARD TO INDIANS

"I can't wait to see everything," said Wendy. "But most of all, I want to see the Mermaids. Can we go to Mermaid Lagoon first?"

"I'd rather see the Indians," said John. His face fell.

"Me, too," agreed Michael.

"Never Never Land's the place where everyone does as he wants," said Peter Pan with a smile. "So here's what we'll do. I'll take Wendy to Mermaid Lagoon. John, you, Michael and the Lost Boys can go out and capture a few Indians. You can be the leader, John."

John beamed with joy. "I'll try to be the best leader ever," he said.

He stepped in front of the other boys and called out, "Forward March. Onward to Indians!"

Michael and the Lost Boys followed. And as they

followed, they sang:

> We're following the leader, the leader,
>   the leader.
> We're following the leader, whatever he
>   may do.
> And since John is the leader, the leader,
>   the leader.
> And since John is the leader, we will
>   follow you.

John led his group a merry, winding way. They went over hills and dales, plains and prairies. Once John led everybody single file over a fallen tree bridge. Another time they ducked behind a waterfall. John led so well no one got wet. Still another time they hopped from stone to stone to cross a roaring stream.

Going into the deep jungle was fun, too. There everyone made monkey faces and swung on the vines.

Finally John led his group through some high grass into a clearing.

Suddenly John stopped short. He bent down to look at some footprints in the mud. He examined them carefully.

"Aha!" he said to the others. "Indians! Big feet. They look like a savage tribe."

"Let's get 'em!" Foxy called out eagerly.

"Let's go!" shouted the others.

"Gentlemen, wait," said John, holding up his hand. "First we must plan our strategy."

"Huh?" asked Cubby. "What's 'strategy'?"

"A plan," said John, who liked long words. "In this case, a plan of attack. And our plan is first to surround the Indians, and then to attack." He circled the footprints with his fingers.

While John went on about his plan, little Michael explored.

He found some interesting things in his wanderings. First he found a strange fancy feather on the ground. Then he saw some walking trees with two feet instead of a trunk—and moccasins on those two feet.

Little Michael hurried back to the huddled boys. He pulled on John's sleeve.

"Indians!" he whispered. "I think I saw Indian trees."

But John was too busy talking to listen. Besides he thought Michael was too little to listen to, which was, of course, foolish.

John was saying, "The Indian is clever and cunning. But not as clever and cunning as we are. What we have to do is surround the Indians. The most important thing is surprise . . . ."

John no sooner got the word "surprise" out than a tree reached out and grabbed him. The tree's leafy arms pulled John into its branches and covered his mouth. He couldn't even call for help.

Other Indians disguised as trees pounced on the other boys. Soon all were captured and made to march back to Indian Camp.

There each boy was tied to a totem pole in front of the campfire.

John felt miserable. He felt he'd failed as leader. "I'm sorry, friends," he said. "It's all my fault."

"Aw, that's okay," said Foxy with a smile. "You couldn't help it." He didn't sound a bit worried.

Now the Indian Chief's large shadow fell on his prisoners. "How!" said the Chief, raising his hand. He wore full feathers and war paint.

"How!" the Lost Boys answered back. None of them sounded scared or worried either. John was completely baffled.

"Ugh!" everyone said as the tomtoms beat loudly.

The Chief beat his chest. "Sometimes you win. Sometimes we win," he said.

"Okay, okay," Foxy called out. "You win this time, Chief. So cut the small talk and cut us loose."

"How come?" John whispered to Foxy. "You mean this is only a game?"

"Sure," said Foxy with a shrug. "When we win, we turn them loose. And when they win, they turn us loose. That way it's fair."

"This time no turn 'em loose," the Chief glared. His face was set and unsmiling.

"Ha, ha, ha," laughed Foxy, "Big Chief is big joker."

"Me no joke!" said the Chief sharply. Then he turned on John and asked, "Where you hide Tiger Lily?"

John didn't answer. He didn't even know who Tiger Lily was.

"The Indian Princess. The Chief's daughter," Foxy told him.

John then spoke to the Chief. "We don't have any princess, honest Indian."

"Honest Indian, ha!" the Chief thundered. "Me think what you say is heap big lie. I say if Tiger Lily not back by sunset, burn 'em at stake."

"All of 'em," he muttered as he stalked off. "Me no joke."

No one thought he was—not even the Lost Boys now.

CHAPTER 8:
AT MERMAID LAGOON

Peter and Wendy were feeling carefree as they neared Mermaid Lagoon. They had no way of knowing the bad news about the boys.

Wendy saw the lagoon from afar—a shapeless pool of lovely pale colors. "Oh," she sighed, "it's even more beautiful than I imagined."

Peter flew on ahead. Mermaids were lolling on all the rocks in the lagoon. "Hello, Peter," they called out as he came nearer.

One was sunning herself. Another was combing her hair and looking at herself in a sea chanty on a trumpet-shell horn.

Two were playing a gentle game with rainbow bubbles. They tried to see who could keep her rainbow bubble in the air longest without it bursting.

Peter landed on top of a large rock. "Hello,"

girls," he called down. "Did you miss me?"

They all nodded "Yes." Then they begged, "Tell us a story, Peter. Something really exciting."

"How about the time I cut off Hook's hand and tossed it to the crocodile?" asked Peter.

The mermaids splashed happily. "Yes, that one," they all said.

Peter began, "It happened like this. There I was on Marooner's Rock surrounded by forty or fifty pirates. Just then . . . ."

"Who's *she*?" One of the mermaids pointed to Wendy, who was just climbing up onto the rocks.

"That's Wendy, my friend," said Peter with a big smile.

"She's a *girl*!" said the mermaid, making it sound like something terrible to be. "What's a *girl* doing here?"

"And in her nightdress, too," sneered a second mermaid.

Wendy saw the mermaids. She thought they were lovely, but she didn't like the nasty looks they were giving her.

"Come on, Dearie," coaxed the mermaid with the seashell comb. "Come join us for a nice swim." She slithered up the rock and tugged at Wendy's long gown.

"Please don't!" said Wendy sharply. "I'm not

dressed for swimming."

"I insist," said the mermaid.

All the mermaids smiled and started thrashing the water and splashing Wendy.

They thought it was great sport. So did Peter Pan.

Wendy didn't. She didn't like getting wet, and she didn't like being splashed. Not one bit.

Wendy picked up a clam shell. "If any of you come closer, I'm going to throw this," she threatened. "And I mean it!"

Peter Pan leaped into the air and took the shell from Wendy's hand. "They're only teasing," he said.

This made Wendy mad. "You call trying to drown me just teasing?" said Wendy angrily. She stamped her foot. "They're jealous because I'm a real girl and they're not!"

Peter didn't know what to say.

Wendy went on. "And if you think I'm going to put up with that kind of nonsense. . . ."

She never had a chance to finish. Peter's expression changed suddenly. He put a hand over her mouth and whispered, "Shhhhhhhsh!"

Peter thought he heard the soft splash of oars. He crouched down and peeked through a crack in the rocky ledge.

He was right! There *was* a rowboat. And Smee, Captain Hook, and Tiger Lily were in it.

"Hook's here!" Peter warned the mermaids.

"Hook," they murmured uneasily. One by one they dove into the deep water. They didn't trust Captain Hook any more than Peter Pan did.

"Hook's captured Tiger Lily," Peter whispered to Wendy. "They're heading by Skull Rock toward Marooner's Rock."

"Stay here," said Peter. "I'm going to see what they're up to." He flew down and hid behind a sea-grape bush.

The rowboat was just rounding the bend. Captain Hook was twirling his mustache and saying, "Now my dear princess, this is my proposition. You tell me where Peter Pan is hiding. And I set you free."

"Am I not a man of my word, Smee?" Hook turned to his first mate.

"Always, Captain," nodded Smee.

"So you'd better talk, my dear," Captain Hook continued in his most silky voice. "Because soon it will be too late. Because soon you will be sitting on Marooner's Rock, and the tide waters will be rising higher and higher."

Tiger Lily turned her head away from the wily pirate captain. She behaved proudly in spite of her fear.

"That old codfish!" said Peter Pan to himself. He always called his longtime enemy that when he was about to have some fun with him.

Peter flew to a rock just behind the rowboat and hid. "Me Manatoa, great spirit of mighty sea water," he called out in a deep Indian voice. "Me speak."

Smee stopped rowing. He looked around nervously. The voice was scary, and Smee scared easily.

Captain Hook drew his sword. "Stand by me, Smee," he commanded. "It's an evil spirit. I'm going to step ashore and look around."

The Captain stepped out toward the very rock where Peter was hiding. Peter darted away in the nick of time.

He flew behind another rock not far from Smee. This time he impersonated Captain Hook's voice. "Mr. Smee," he said, just as Hook might have said it, "do as I say."

"Wh-wh-what is it, Captain?" the first mate was all shivery with fear. The voice sounded like Hook's. But both his eyes and the fog were so bad he couldn't really see the person speaking.

The voice went on, "Release the princess and take her back to her people. I'll stay here. These are my orders."

Smee saluted into the fog bank. "Aye, Aye, Sir,

I've got you."

Smee readied his oars and started to row away.

Captain Hook saw what was going on. He raced down the bank and pulled the boat back with his foot. "By my blarmy, what do you think you're doing?" he bellowed.

"Just what you told me," said Smee. "I'm carrying out orders."

"My orders!" Hook raged. "What orders?"

"Y-y-you said to take Tiger Lily back," Smee stuttered.

"You blithering idiot!" snorted the captain. He slashed the air just above Smee's head. Then he leaped back into the rowboat.

Peter Pan watched, doubled up with laughter.

Then he got right in the thick of it. He flew through the fog and snatched the hat off Hook's head. He took his pistol, too, and dropped it in Smee's lap.

"Let him have it," Peter said again imitating Captain Hook's voice.

Bang! Bang! Smee shot twice. Only the person who almost had it was Captain Hook. Fortunately for the pirate, Smee's aim was as bad as his eyes.

"What a pity!" Peter now spoke in his own voice.

Captain Hook grabbed back his hat as Peter whizzed by. "Scurvy brat!" he called out.

"Thank you, Captain," smiled Peter.

"Come on back if you've a taste for blood," Hook called after him.

Peter did. The two of them had a real battle right there in the rowboat. The Captain sliced the air with his sword. Peter Pan ducked and ducked and crowed with delight.

This infuriated the captain, who lunged so far out on one mighty thrust that he fell—*kersplash*—into the water.

Too late Captain Hook heard a faint tick-tock, tick-tock. "The croc's in the water with me!" he called as he thrashed wildly.

Snap! The crocodile grabbed Captain Hook by the coattail.

The captain, slipping out of his coat, pulled himself up on a rock ledge. The crocodile went snapping and snorting after him. One nip and it wanted the whole of Hook.

Now Captain Hook's foot slipped. He fell off the rock right into the crocodile's wide open mouth.

Shaking and quaking in fear he stood with his hands on the beast's upper teeth and his feet on the lower. Keeping the crocodile's mouth wide open was the only way he could think of to keep from being eaten.

This made the crocodile mad. It rolled its eyes

and lashed its tail.

When the tip of the tail hit Captain Hook, he flew into the air and landed smack on the crocodile's snout. He slid down it like a water chute and splashed into the water.

The captain started swimming for dear life, with the croc only inches behind. He swam all the way back to the pirate ship. Peter Pan crowed for the fun of it.

"Aren't you forgetting something, Peter?" Wendy called down from the ledge where she'd been watching and waiting. She wanted to go on with the tour of Never Never Land.

"I sure did," said Peter, taking to the air.

But Peter misunderstood. Instead of picking up Wendy, he swooped down and picked up Tiger Lily. Peter had to take Tiger Lily back to the Indian village.

"Wait for me!" Wendy called as the two of them flew off together. But they didn't, and she didn't like it. No one likes being left behind.

CHAPTER 9:
A PLAN AND A PARTY

Captain Hook got back to the pirate ship no worse for his scare. But he was in a bad mood. He also had the sniffles and the shivers from being in the water so long.

Back in his captain's cabin, he held his head and wailed, "Peter Pan made a fool of me. Owwww!"

There was a knock on the door. Starkey, one of the pirate crew, came in carrying a tray. "Hot water for your tea," he said to his ailing commander.

Smee took the tray—and in taking it, he turned around and smacked Captain Hook hard in his aching head. Smee was such a bungler. Captain Hook slumped in his chair and had a funny, dazed look on his face.

Poor nearsighted Smee. He didn't realize what he'd just done. He thought the captain was smiling.

"Seeing you smile brings back the good old days," Smee babbled to his captain. "Why don't we put to sea again? Sinking ships and cutting throats are such fun!"

Smee leaned over and whispered in the captain's ear, "You know there's trouble on the Island. Woman trouble. Cook told me that second mate told him that Peter Pan banished Tinker Bell forever!"

The news revived Captain Hook. He sprang to his feet, saying, "Ho, ho, ho! Did you say Peter Pan banished Tinker Bell?" He felt so much better he swung Smee around and did a little dance.

"Aye, aye, Captain," said Smee.

"Why?" asked Captain Hook with an evil smirk.

"On account of Wendy," said Smee. "Tinker Bell tried to do Wendy in, she did."

"Oooooooo! That's terrible!" Captain Hook smiled and crossed all his fingers and toes.

"Well," Smee explained, "Tink's terrible jealous." Once more he pleaded, "Can't we set to sea again? Port's no place for a real pirate.

"You're right, Smee," agreed Captain Hook, "as you seldom are. Get my dress coat. The sooner we get out of here the better."

"Aye, aye, sir!" beamed Smee.

Captain Hook sniggered to himself. "Ah ha! Ho ho! A jealous person can be tricked into anything. All I have to do is make Tinker Bell think we want to help *her*. Then she'll chart our course to Peter Pan."

Smee was halfway out the door when Captain Hook called, "Where do you think you're going?"

"To tell the boys we sail with the tide," said Smee.

"Not so fast," Captain Hook pulled Smee back with his hook hand. "You will go ashore first. Pick up Tinker Bell and bring her back to me. Or else."

Smee didn't exactly understand. But he did as he was asked. The captain's "or else's" were too terrible to think about.

While Captain Hook was plotting and planning, the Indians were celebrating Tiger Lily's safe return. The tomtoms were beating. A big ceremony was going on.

The Big Chief was decked out in full war paint and festive feathers.

"You mighty brave warrior," he praised Peter Pan. "You now Little Flying Eagle." As he said it, he put a fancy feathered headdress on Peter's head.

Peter whooped for joy. John and Michael and the Lost Boys cheered too, "Hooray for Peter Pan!"

Wendy was the only one who didn't cheer. She felt left out and unhappy. Besides her feelings were still hurt because Peter picked up Tiger Lily and left her behind. She sat back as everyone passed the peace pipe. And she only half-heartedly joined in the chanting and dancing.

"Everyone's having fun but me!" thought Wendy sadly. Tiger Lily was dancing with Peter Pan and John was yelling "Wahoo!"

The last straw was when little Michael spun by and tossed Wendy his teddy bear. "Takem papoose," he said.

"Wendy no takem *any* more," Wendy stamped her foot and stalked off. She wanted to take a long walk. Never Never Land wasn't all wonderful, she decided.

CHAPTER 10:
TINKER BELL TRAPPED

Tinker Bell heard the party noises, too. She was in a bad mood, and her light was not at all bright.

"Begging your pardon, Miss Bell," said Smee, suddenly appearing under the branch where Tink was sitting. "Captain Hook would like a word with you."

"Why not!" Tinker Bell shrugged her tiny shoulders. She had to talk to someone.

Captain Hook was in his quarters playing the piano when Tinker Bell was brought in. He was wearing his shirt with lace cuffs and fanciest pirate finery.

"Good evening, Miss Bell," he got up and bowed. "I'm *very* glad to see you."

He leaned down to Tinker Bell and whispered in a low voice, "I am a defeated man. Tomorrow I leave Never Never Land never to return."

"It's true," sobbed Smee. "That's what I'm here to tell the crew."

"And that's why I asked you over, my dear," said Captain Hook in his most oily manner. "I just want you to know that I bear Peter Pan no ill will, none at all."

Tinker Bell turned up her tiny nose at the mention of Peter's name. But she clung to every word.

"Oh, Peter has his faults to be sure," Captain Hook tried to sound casual, "like bringing that Wendy to the Island, for instance."

Tinker Bell jangled loudly at the sound of Wendy's name.

"Dangerous business that!" Captain Hook glanced slyly at her. "Why, rumor has it that she made trouble between you and Peter."

Now Tink was burning. Tiny jeweled tears sparkled and fell from her eyes.

"What's this?" asked Captain Hook, oozing charm. "Tears? My dear, how tragic. It makes me sad to see you so unhappy."

Tinker Bell was sobbing so hard she didn't see the smirk on Hook's face as he added, "Then it's true. Peter Pan cast you aside—like an old glove!" He tossed his gloves on the cabin floor just to make the point.

"But we mustn't judge Peter too harshly," Captain Hook handed his handkerchief to Tinker Bell. "Especially when it's *Wendy* who's to blame!"

He let his words sink in, then turned to Smee. "Smee," the captain said, "we must help Tinker Bell and save Peter Pan from himself."

"How!" asked Smee between sobs.

"We'll sail in the morning," said Hook. "And when we sail, we'll take Wendy with us. It's the only answer."

Tinker Bell dried her tears and nodded.

"With Wendy gone, Peter will soon come to his senses," said Captain Hook. "He'll remember his true and devoted little friend here."

The captain put his hook hand around Tinker Bell and sighed, "Ah, what a kindness we will have done!"

Tinker Bell's tinkle sounded lighter and happier.

Hook then stood up. "Smee!" he ordered, "we must leave as soon as possible. It's high time we do our good deed. We'll surround Peter's home. Undoubtedly the Wendy creature will be there."

"B-b-but Captain," sputtered Smee. "We don't know where Peter Pan lives."

"By my blarmy, you're right," Captain Hook winked. "We don't know where Peter lives."

Tinker Bell overheard. She flapped her wings and flew up on Captain Hook's shoulder. She tinkled something in his ear.

"What's that, my dear?" Captain Hook smiled. "*You* could show us the way. Why I *never* thought of that!"

The wily captain shoved Smee a pencil and paper. "Take this down," he ordered.

Tinker Bell knew a better way. She dipped her dainty toes into the captain's ink bottle. Then she flew to his large pirate map.

She made her marks on the map, and the captain put them in words. "I see," he said. "Start at Pegleg Point. Then go forty paces west of Blindman's Bluff."

"I've got it!" Hook jumped up. "Just a hop and a skip across Crocodile Creek. Then north by northeast. . . ."

All at once Tinker Bell stopped writing. A worried look crossed her face.

She flew over to Hook and hovered in front of him.

"Continue, my dear," he urged.

Tinker Bell didn't. She just looked at Captain Hook pleadingly and tinkled softly.

"I mustn't harm Peter?" the captain asked. "Is that what you're trying to tell me?"

Tinker Bell shook her head "Yes."

"Madam," said Hook, crossing his hook in his fingers, "Captain Hook gives his word not to lay a hand, or a hook, on Peter Pan."

Tinker Bell looked relieved. She flew back to the map and made a last mark at Hangman's Tree. Then she stopped.

"Hangman's Tree!" said Captain Hook. "So that's the secret entrance to Peter's hiding place.

"Thank you, my dear," he added sweetly. "You have been most helpful."

He held out his hook hand to shake Tinker Bell's tiny one.

Instead, he snatched Tinker Bell and tossed her into the ship's lantern. He'd gotten what he wanted. And it was as good a cage as any.

CHAPTER 11:
AMBUSHED

The party for Peter Pan was still going on at the Indian Camp when Wendy returned from her walk. "Big Chief Little Flying Eagle greets you," crowed Peter.

"Ugh!" said Wendy huffily. She was still feeling hurt and left out. And something else—she was beginning to be a bit homesick.

"Is that all you have to say?" asked Peter. Now he looked hurt. "Everyone else thinks I'm wonderful."

"Especially Tiger Lily," said Wendy sourly. She turned from Peter and walked over to John and Michael. John was beating his top hat like a tom-tom. Michael was whooping it up around it.

"Michael Darling," said Wendy sternly, "take off that war paint at once and get ready for bed."

Little Michael folded his arms stubbornly. "Braves no sleep," he said. "Braves go days without sleep."

"But you're a *boy* not a brave," said Wendy somewhat crossly. "You're a boy, and I think we all should go home."

"Me no want to go home," said Michael.

"You no go home," Peter Pan shook his feathered head. "You stay many moons. We have heap good time."

"Now Peter," said Wendy, trying to reason, "let's stop pretending and be practical."

Peter Pan shuddered. "No like practical. Little Flying Eagle has spoken."

Wendy stamped her foot and said, "Oh, Peter, for goodness sake, please. . . ."

But it was no use. So she turned to John. At least he was a real boy. He might understand.

Wendy asked, "John, do you want to stay here and grow up like a little savage?"

"Why not!" grinned John.

"But you *can't!*" said Wendy, almost in tears. "You need a mother. We all do."

"Aren't you our mother, Wendy?" asked little Michael.

Wendy was shocked. "Why, Michael, of cours not!" she said. "Surely you haven't forgotten our real mother!"

"Did she have silky ears and wear a fur coat?" asked Michael eagerly.

Wendy looked sad. She put her arms around Michael. "That wasn't your *real* mother," she said. "That was your nursemaid, Nana. Nana the dog, remember?"

It was clear Michael didn't.

All the talk stirred some long lost memory in Cubby. "I think I had a mother—once," he said.

"What was she like?" asked one twin.

"What was she like?" repeated the other twin.

"I forget," said Cubby, scratching his head. He thought a while and said, "I had a white rat once. Is that like a mother?"

"How would you know if you can't remember?" snarled Foxy. All this talk about something he didn't have made him feel nervous. It was like hearing about a party and not being invited. To change the subject, he punched Cubby in the nose. Soon all the Lost Boys were fussing and fighting.

"Stop it at once!" shouted Wendy. "I'll tell you what a mother is," she said gently. She lifted little Michael onto her lap and sang:

> She's the angel voice that bids you good night,
> kisses your cheek and whispers sleep tight.
> She's the helping hand that guides you along,
> Whether you're right, whether you're wrong.
> Just ask your heart to tell you her worth,

And your heart will say heaven on earth.
For no one other is like your mother.

This only made things worse. Now all the Lost
Boys knew what they were missing. No one spoke a
work when Wendy had finished.

Even Peter Pan felt something he didn't understand. It was like a terrible lump in the throat.

Michael broke the silence. "I want my mother,"
he sobbed. And this started everyone crying
—everyone but Peter. He went to a far corner of the
cave to sulk. He didn't want to hear another word
about mothers. Or any grown-ups.

It was the perfect opportunity for Captain Hook's
pirate crew to surround the cave entrance.

This they did, unknown to Wendy or the boys,
who were too deep in thought to listen for footsteps.

Suddenly John got up on a chair. He waved his
umbrella and said, "I propose we leave for home at
once!"

"Can I come too?" begged Cubby.

"Take us along," said the twins. "Please, Wendy," all the Lost Boys pleaded.

"I don't think my mother would mind," said
Wendy, "if Peter doesn't." She turned to him.

"Go on!" said Peter Pan. He sounded sad and
miserable. "See if I care! Go back and grow up if

that's what you want."

He felt betrayed. "But I'm warning you," he said to the Lost Boys, "once you're grown up, you can never come back to Never Never Land. Never!" he repeated.

"Who cares!" said Cubby. "Let's go."

John was still the leader, so he led the group. "Men, Wendy, shall we be off?" he pointed toward the cave entrance. He raised his umbrella as a signal to go.

Everyone marched single file behind John. Only Peter Pan stayed behind. He went back to his corner, played his pipes, and sulked some more. "They'll be back," he said to himself.

Wendy felt sorry for Peter. She stayed behind and said softly, "Goodbye, Peter Pan."

Peter kept on playing his pipes. He didn't even look at her. Finally Wendy waved and followed after the others—up the winding dirt path to the cave entrance. She hated to leave Peter. But she wanted to go home. It was a terrible fix.

What she didn't know was that, one by one, the clever pirates had ambushed her brothers and the Lost Boys. They had caught them all off guard.

Like the others, Wendy was grabbed and gagged at the cave entrance. She didn't have a chance to scream.

Peter Pan, still sulking inside the cave, never knew his friends had been captured. They couldn't come back even if they wanted to. Instead of being homeward bound, they were bound and gagged, and being taken to Captain Hook's pirate ship.

CHAPTER 12:
A PIRATE PLAN

C aptain Hook stood on the deck of his ship and eyed the motley group of prisoners before him. Only Peter Pan was missing.

The captain chuckled to himself. Even that didn't matter much. He held the answer to Peter Pan in his hand, in a large square clock-size box.

"And now, Smee," said the captain curling his lip, "here's a present for Peter Pan. Hop in the rowboat and take it to him at once."

Smee heard the ticks and the tocks coming from the box. He knew it was a powerful time bomb. "Wouldn't it be more human-like just to slit his throat?" said Smee with a shudder.

"Aye, that it would," snickered Captain Hook. "But I gave my word not to lay a finger or a hook on Peter Pan. Heh, heh, heh! And Captain Hook never breaks a promise."

"Yo, ho, yo," his crew laughed with him. As Smee

101

left, they burst into song:

> Oh, a pirate's life is a happy life.
> You can sample the life of a crook.
> There isn't a boy who wouldn't enjoy
> working for dear Captain Hook,
> the world's most infamous crook.

"Flattery," Captain Hook beamed. "How I love it." He was so happy he did a little dance on the poop deck.

Afterwards, he turned to his prisoners. "I'll tell you what I'll do," he told them, pointing to a large, open book. "To all of you who sign up right away to be on my crew, I'll give a free tattoo. How kind of me!" sighed Captain Hook.

"Yo, ho, ho," the crew heartily agreed. They waved their pirate flags and sang to their prisoners:

> Oh, you'll love the life of a thief.
> You'll relish the life of a crook.
> There's a barrel of fun
> for everyone,
> and you'll get treasure
> by the ton.
> So step up and sign the book.
> Join up with Captain Hook.

Everyone was convinced but Wendy. Soon as their ropes were cut, John, Michael and the Lost Boys ran up pell-mell to sign the book.

"Boys!" Wendy yelled at the top of her lungs. They all skidded to a stop.

"Aren't you ashamed of yourselves?" she scolded.

"I'd rather be a pirate than walk the plank," said John very logically. He was always practical.

"I-I-I can't swim," sobbed Michael. He clutched his teddy bear. Even it looked scared.

"None of us will walk the plank," whispered Wendy with more courage than she felt. "Peter Pan will save us. I just know it."

Captain Hook overheard. So did Smee, who was just returning to the ship from the rowboat. They both laughed till their sides ached.

"A thousand pardons, my dear," said Captain Hook. "I don't believe you are in on our little joke."

"What little joke?" asked Wendy.

Hook moved in closer. "Smee left a little present for Peter Pan," he said confidentially. "Something to take your place."

"Sort of a surprise present," added Smee gleefully. "Why I can almost see him reading the card now, 'To Peter with love from Wendy. Do not open till six o'clock. Sharp.' "

"But I didn't send Peter anything!" protested

Wendy.

"Of course *you* didn't," smirked Captain Hook. "I did. That nice little square box you saw. Inside is a nice little time bomb set exactly for six."

"Oh, no!" cried Wendy.

"Oh, yes!" Captain Hook winked wickedly. "When Peter opens his present, he'll be blasted out of Never Never Land forever."

He looked at his watch. "Time grows short," said Captain Hook. "We've less than a minute to wait."

While Captain Hook was looking at his watch, Tinker Bell was breaking out of her lantern cage. Pure fury gave her the strength to bend the bars.

She flew away from the ship, straight to Peter Pan's cave hideaway.

When she got there, Peter was holding his present and looking pleased.

"Look, Tink," he said, holding up the package. "It's a present from Wendy." He was smiling for the first time in a long time. In his joy, he'd forgotten about his fight with Tinker Bell.

He read her the sweet card, "To Peter with love from Wendy. Do not open till six o'clock. Sharp."

Peter looked at the cave clock. It was half a minute till six.

"I guess I can open it now," said Peter. "I can't wait to see what's inside. It ticks, too."

Eagerly he ripped off the ribbon and wrapping paper. He was just about to open the box when Tinker Bell tinkled furiously.

It was then that Peter Pan remembered how jealous Tink had been of Wendy.

Tinker Bell tried to grab the box. "Oh, no, you don't," said Peter, putting it behind him. "You should be ashamed of yourself, trying to snatch Wendy's present."

Tinker Bell jingled and jangled louder than ever. Only ten seconds were left.

"Stop it, Tink!" Peter scolded. "Don't be so silly. You act as if there's a time bomb in here."

Tinker Bell didn't think it was silly. She saw the square box start to smoke. She knew what was inside.

With a mighty effort she dove at the box and knocked it out of Peter's hand. Then she threw her tiny self on top of it and pushed it as far as possible from Peter.

BOOM! There was a thunderous explosion that shook all of Never Never Land. Then there was silence.

The big boom was heard far out at sea, on the pirate ship.

"And so I lose a worthy opponent," said Captain Hook. He took off his pirate hat and hung his head in mock sorrow.

Wendy and the boys were speechless with real sorrow. They were sure Peter Pan was dead.

CHAPTER 13:
WALKING THE PLANK

Thanks to brave tiny Tinker Bell, Peter Pan was not dead. He was merely shaken.

"So it *was* a bomb!" said Peter weakly. "And Tink knew it all the time."

The first thing he did was search for her. The cave was dark and filled with dust. He couldn't see her light at all, which was not a good sign.

"Tink! Tinker Bell, where are you?" Peter called frantically.

Finally he found her under a pile of rubble. Her light was so faint it was almost out. "Are you all right?" asked Peter. "Please be all right, Tink."

Tinker Bell tinkled weakly. She told Peter everything—how she'd been so jealous she'd betrayed him, and how sorry she was, and how Wendy and the boys had been captured.

Peter could see her light growing fainter with each tinkle. "Don't say any more," he said with tears in his eyes. "You are my first and best friend, and you mean more to me than anyone, even Wendy. Believe me."

His touching words made Tinker Bell better. Gradually her glow grew stronger. She was saved.

While Tinker Bell was recovering, Captain Hook, that vile villain, was making his last offer.

He held up a plume pen. "So which will it be?" he sneered. "The pen or the plank?"

Wendy took the pen. She held it mid-air and let out a stream of ink—straight at Captain Hook's clean white shirt.

"We will never join your pirate crew!" she said staunchly.

"As you wish," said Captain Hook. He made a sweeping bow. "Ladies first," he murmured, pointing to the plank.

"Goodbye, John. Goodbye, Michael. Goodbye, boys," Wendy tried to be brave.

"Goodbye, Wendy," they waved back.

"Come on, girl. Quit lollygagging," said a rude pirate as he gave Wendy a shove.

Wendy kept her head up and her eyes straight ahead as she walked the length of the plank. She walked slowly and thought sad thoughts about never seeing her mother or father or Nana again.

At the end of the plank, she hesitated. It was such

a long way down, and there was no returning.

And then she plunged.

"That's funny," said Captain Hook afterwards.

"Not a sound. Nary a splash."

"Right," said Smee, stroking his chin. "Not a blooming ripple."

"It's a jinx," said the pirate Starkey. "There should have been a splash."

"The ship's bewitched," the other pirates started murmuring.

The murmurs got back to Captain Hook. "So you want a splash do you," he snarled. "Well, I'll give you one."

He took his hook hand and hurled Starkey over the ship's railing.

"Who's next?" he asked.

"You are. And here I am," an all-too-familiar voice answered.

Captain Hook followed the sound of the voice. He could hardly believe his eyes. There on the anchor chair was Peter Pan with Wendy in his arms!

Then Peter flew with Wendy up to the crow's nest. Tinker Bell flitted behind.

Smee clung to the ship's railing. "It-it-it can't be," he stammered. "It's his blinking ghost." Smee's eyes were wide as saucers.

"Say your prayers, Hook," crowed Peter Pan. "I'll show you this ghost has blood in his veins."

Peter drew his knife and dove down at Captain Hook.

110

"I'll run you through," cried Captain Hook. "Take that!"

"Missed by a mile," laughed Peter Pan.

Enraged at being laughed at, Captain Hook lashed wildly with his hook hand. The hook part of it sunk into the mast and stuck there.

This gave Peter the chance he was waiting for. Quickly he flew to the boys and freed them. He cut all their ropes and called, "Follow me. Climb the rigging. It's your best escape."

John, Michael and the Lost Boys clambered across the cannon and down the deck after Peter. On the way, they picked up as many cannon balls as they could carry, just in case the pirates chased after them.

Little Michael had the hardest time. He was trying to carry a cannon ball *and* his teddy bear, and it was too much for him.

"Hurry, Michael," said John. "Hold on to my umbrella and give me the cannon ball." He tucked it under his nightshirt. Then he pulled Michael up the rigging.

"Don't stand there, you bilge rats!" Captain Hook thundered at his crew. They were standing motionless. "Stop watching me and get those scurvy brats!"

The crew was startled into action. They raced

across the deck and started up the rigging.

But they weren't quite quick enough. The boys were already in the crow's nest with Peter and Wendy.

It was still a dangerous situation. The pirates kept on climbing. They came closer and closer.

When one of them got within inches of little Michael's foot, John gave the command: "Ready . . . Aim . . . Fire!"

The boys rained down cannon balls and anything they had in their pockets. The pirates fell back. Some even jumped in fear into the water.

Peter Pan crowed and flew back down on deck, right in front of Captain Hook. Peter was feeling pretty cocky, which was just what Captain Hook couldn't stand about him.

With an angry yank, Captain Hook finally jerked loose. His hook was free. But he fell over backwards into the sea—smack! right on the waiting crocodile's snout.

The crocodile was so surprised, its jaws snapped shut. It missed its big chance, and Captain Hook bounded back on deck.

Now Captain Hook fairly twitched to get Peter. The captain went after his enemy full fury. He slashed with his sword and swiped with his hook.

But he never came close. Every time Captain

Hook thought he had him, Peter flew off somewhere else.

"This is no mere boy fighting me!" cried the pirate captain. "This is a fiend, a flying devil."

He was made madder by the children clapping and calling from the crow's nest, "Hooray," and "Hit Hook again, harder!"

Finally Captain Hook could stand it no longer. "You coward!" he called to Peter Pan.

"Me?" Peter sounded surprised.

"Yes, you," raged Captain Hook. "You don't fight fair. You wouldn't dare fight me like a real boy. All you do is flit away like a sparrow."

"Nobody calls me a coward and lives," said Peter Pan. "I can fight you hand to hand with one arm behind my back," he boasted, "and win."

"Promise you won't fly," said Captain Hook. He faced Peter Pan squarely.

"Promise," said Peter.

"Don't!" Wendy called from the crow's nest. "It's a trick. Don't trust him."

"I'll take my chances," said Peter confidently. Then he said to Captain Hook. "All right, I'll fight your way. I give my word I won't fly."

"And I give mine," said Captain Hook. There was a wicked gleam in his eye as he locked swords with Peter Pan.

CHAPTER 14:
HOMEWARD BOUND

Here goes!" cried Captain Hook. He swung his sword hard, calling, "I'll cleave you in the brisket."

Peter ducked just in time. Peter was quick. But Captain Hook was quicker. It was soon clear that the Captain had the advantage. Peter wasn't used to fighting with his feet on the ground.

Once Captain Hook came so close he parted the hair on Peter's head. If Tinker Bell hadn't tweaked the captain's mustache, Peter might have been done in.

The duel continued with the odds in favor of Captain Hook. "The end is near. How delightful," said the captain.

And then it happened. Peter Pan lost his footing. As he stumbled, Captain Hook knocked the sword right out of his hand.

"Prepare to die!" cried Captain Hook. He had

Peter pinned against the mast. His sword wavered in front of Peter's chest.

"Fly!" Wendy called from the crow's nest. She covered her eyes. She couldn't look.

"I can't," said Peter. "I gave my word I wouldn't."

Now that Peter Pan was unarmed, Captain Hook felt confident—so confident that he started waving the big skull and crossbones pirate flag. "Ho ho, ho hee," he bragged. "The victory will soon be mine."

"Don't be so sure," said Peter. Quick as a wink, he flipped the flag over Hook's head.

Peter took Hook's own sword and turned it on the wicked pirate. "Aha!" Peter crowed, "the tables are turned. The victory is mine." It was the game he'd been wanting to win for years!

"Hooray for Peter Pan," Wendy, John and Michael cheered wildly.

What the Lost Boys said wasn't so nice. "Give him one for me," and "Off with his head," and

"Cleave him to the mast."

Peter Pan stood on top of Captain Hook. The sword tip tickled the captain's throat. Peter was enjoying himself immensely.

Captain Hook was not. "You wouldn't do old Hook in, now would you lad?" he asked in a trembling voice.

Peter edged the sword point a little closer.

"I'll go away. I'll do anything you say," sniveled Hook. He was shaking like a leaf.

"Okay," said Peter. He pulled back the sword. "I'll let you go if you'll admit. . ."

"Admit what?" asked Captain Hook anxiously.

"Admit that you're a silly codfish and not a wicked pirate at all," said Peter Pan.

"Impossible!" said Captain Hook. "I have my pride. Especially not in front of the crew," he added confidentially.

But the sword was pressing down on his throat so finally Captain Hook whispered, "I'm *not* a wicked pirate at all. I'm just a silly codfish."

"Louder!" commanded Peter. "I want it heard in the crow's nest."

"I'm just a silly codfish!" Captain Hook screamed it at the top of his lungs.

Soon everybody was chanting, "Captain Hook's a codfish. Captain Hook's a codfish."

Finally Peter said, "Very well. You're free to go—as long as you never ever return to Never Never Land."

"I wouldn't want to," said Captain Hook huffily.

Peter Pan then tossed both swords overboard. But Captain Hook had one last sneaky trick. Instead of leaving, he crept up behind Peter and tried to strike him down with his hook hand.

"Peter, look out," Wendy screamed.

Peter flew out of range. Captain Hook, however, kept on going.

"Owwwwwww!" he went over the ship's side, into the crocodile infested waters.

Tick-tock, tick-tock, the huge hungry crocodile who'd been waiting so long was right there. It rolled its eyes and smacked its lips and went snapping after the floundering captain.

Captain Hook did a fast and furious crawlstroke. "Smee! Mates!" he called to his crew. "To the row-boats! Rescue me!"

Tick-tock, tick-tock, the crocodile was gaining. But he couldn't quite catch up.

Hurriedly Smee and the pirates manned the boats. They raced after their captain, but they couldn't catch up either.

Captain Hook, the crocodile, and the pirate crew were soon out of sight. They disappeared over the horizon. The ship was left to Peter Pan and his friends.

"All right, you swabs," said Peter with a grin, "heave those halyards. Aloft and set sail. We're casting off."

"Where are we going?" asked Wendy.

"To London Town," said Peter with a wink. "To a cozy town house on a quiet street."

Wendy cried for joy, "We're going home! John, Michael, we're really truly going home!"

Tinker Bell tinkled merrily. Now she'd have Peter all to herself again. What a splendid way to get rid of Wendy. Peter Pan had such good ideas.

"Hoist anchor," Peter commanded.

"Aye, aye, Captain," said the new crew of Lost Boys as the anchor chain came up.

Tinker Bell was so happy she dusted the ship's wheel with a fine coating of pixie dust. This made the ship glow and grow lighter, and lift up from the water. They were off.

The strange ship sailed through the night sky—by stars and clouds and playful comets—straight to London. The Darling children climbed back in the nursery window at midnight, just as Big Ben was striking.

John and Michael were so sleepy they went straight to their beds.

Wendy stayed on the window seat and watched. She wanted to wave a last goodbye to Peter Pan. Then she too fell asleep.

Mother and Father Darling got home shortly thereafter.

"George, I'm so glad you changed your mind about Wendy," Mother Darling was saying as she and Father Darling were walking in the door. "After all, she's still a child."

Father Darling was feeling more mellow. "You know I didn't mean all those things I said," he told her. "I never do, do I, Nana?" he asked the big dog, who was happily at his side.

Nana the nursemaid woofed and followed her masters up the stairs. It had been a long night full of strange sights for her. She wanted to check in on the children to make sure they were all right.

Mother Darling was the first one in the nursery. "Oh dear!" she cried out. "Wendy's not in her bed."

She turned up the gaslights. Then she sighed, "Ah, there's Wendy asleep on the window seat. Isn't that sweet!"

Very gently she poked Wendy. "What on earth are you doing here?" she asked.

"Ahhhh! Ummmmmm!" Wendy opened one sleepy eye. She only half woke up.

"Oh, Mother," she sighed happily. "We're back—all except the Lost Boys. They didn't stay after all. It's too late for them here."

"Lost boys ... too late," sputtered Father Darling.

"Yes," said Wendy, sitting up. "That's why they

went back to Never Never Land."

"Never Never Land?" said Father Darling in a voice Wendy had never heard.

Wendy smiled sleepily at her father. "I guess I'm ready to grow up," she said. "In the morning."

"No hurry, my dear," said her father. "All in good time."

"Oh, Father," said Wendy excitedly. "We did have such a good time. We saw Tinker Bell and the mermaids and all the Indians and Captain Hook and his pirates and, of course, Peter Pan. He saved me when I was kidnapped and . . . ."

"Kidnapped!" said Father Darling in a shocked voice.

"Yes," said Wendy. "I was scared only I tried not to show it. Peter Pan rescued me. I always knew he would."

Wendy sighed dreamily. "Then we got rid of the pirates and the crocodile was chasing Captain Hook, and then we sailed right through the night sky to get here."

Wendy paused. "He really is wonderful, isn't he!" she said with feeling.

"He? Who?" asked Father Darling.

As he asked it, Father Darling gazed out the nursery window. Something strange and glowing was hovering just outside. It looked half like a cloud, half like a ship. A boy in green seemed to be at the helm.

"George, look!" said Mother Darling.

"Well, I'll be . . ." said Father Darling in a funny, faraway voice. "I've the oddest feeling I've seen that ship *and* that boy before."

"When?" asked Wendy.

"Where?" asked Mother Darling.

"Oh," said Father Darling, "a long time ago, when I was little like you."

He put his arms around Wendy and Mother Darling. They all hugged each other and were happy.